# Old Bear
## and
# His Cub

*For Johnny . . .*

*from Old Bear*

# Old Bear and His Cub

## Olivier
## Dunrea

**Philomel Books**
An Imprint of Penguin Group (USA) Inc.

Old Bear loved his Little Cub with all his heart.

Little Cub loved Old Bear with all *his* heart.

Every morning they ate breakfast together.

"Eat all your porridge, Little Cub," said Old Bear.

"No, I won't," said Little Cub.

"Yes, you will," said Old Bear.

"No, I won't," said Little Cub.

Old Bear stared hard at Little Cub.

Little Cub ate his porridge.

All of it.

Old Bear and Little Cub trudged through the snow.

Old Bear rolled in the snow.

Little Bear rolled in the snow.

"Tie your scarf tight around your neck. You might catch a cold," said Old Bear.

"No, I won't," said Little Cub.

"Yes, you will," said Old Bear.

"No, I won't," said Little Cub.

Old Bear and Little Cub stared hard at each other.

"Hmpff!" said Little Cub.

Old Bear and Little Cub hiked through the woods.

Little Cub climbed to the top of a craggy rock.

"Be careful not to fall, Little Cub," said Old Bear.

"I won't," said Little Cub.

"Yes, you will," said Old Bear.

"No, I won't," said Little Cub.

Old Bear stared hard at Little Cub.

Little Cub slowly climbed down.

All the way.

Old Bear and Little Cub lay down in a snowy meadow
to take a nap.

Little Cub stood on his head and waggled his feet.

"Go to sleep, Little Cub," said Old Bear.

"No, I won't," said Little Cub.

"Yes, you will," said Old Bear.

"No, I won't," said Little Cub.

Old Bear and Little Cub snuffled nose to nose.

Little Cub curled up against Old Bear and closed his eyes.

Fast asleep.

Old Bear loved his Little Cub with all his heart.

Little Cub loved Old Bear with all *his* heart.

Old Bear and Little Cub headed for home.

Old Bear sneezed.

"Bless you," said Little Cub. "You need a scarf so you don't catch a cold."

"I won't," said Old Bear.

"Yes, you will," said Little Cub.

"No, I won't," said Old Bear.

Little Cub stared hard at Old Bear.

"Hmpff!" said Old Bear.

Old Bear loved his Little Cub with all his heart.

Little Cub loved Old Bear with all *his* heart.

Old Bear and Little Cub stamped the snow off their feet.

Old Bear shivered and shook the snow off his fur.

Little Cub danced and shook the snow off his fur.

Old Bear sneezed again.

"Bless you," said Little Cub.

"Thank you," said Old Bear.

"You'll feel better if you crawl into bed," said Little Cub.

"No, I won't," said Old Bear.

"Yes, you will," said Little Cub.

"No, I won't," said Old Bear.

Little Cub stared hard at Old Bear.

Old Bear shivered and crawled into bed.

Snug under the covers,

Old Bear sneezed and blew his nose.

Little Cub brewed some blackberry tea and

put in lots of honey.

"Drink this tea. You'll feel better," said Little Cub.

"No, I won't," said Old Bear.

"Yes, you will," said Little Cub.

"No, I won't," said Old Bear.

Little Cub stared hard at Old Bear.

Old Bear drank the blackberry tea.

All of it.

Old Bear loved his Little Cub with all his heart.

Little Cub loved Old Bear with all *his* heart.

Little Cub read to Old Bear all through the night.

Little Cub yawned.

He crawled into bed beside Old Bear.

Old Bear put his arm around Little Cub.

Little Cub snuggled close.

"I do feel better, Little Cub," said Old Bear.

"So do I," whispered Little Cub.

Little Cub fell fast asleep.

"Good night, Little Cub," said Old Bear.

Old Bear kissed Little Cub on the top of his head.

And he held his little cub all through the night.

Patricia Lee Gauch, Editor

PHILOMEL BOOKS
A division of Penguin Young Readers Group.   Published by The Penguin Group.
Penguin Group (USA) Inc., 375 Hudson Street, New York, NY 10014, U.S.A.
Penguin Group (Canada), 90 Eglinton Avenue East, Suite 700, Toronto, Ontario M4P 2Y3, Canada
    (a division of Pearson Penguin Canada Inc.).
Penguin Books Ltd, 80 Strand, London WC2R 0RL, England.
Penguin Ireland, 25 St. Stephen's Green, Dublin 2, Ireland (a division of Penguin Books Ltd).
Penguin Group (Australia), 250 Camberwell Road, Camberwell, Victoria 3124, Australia
    (a division of Pearson Australia Group Pty Ltd).
Penguin Books India Pvt Ltd, 11 Community Centre, Panchsheel Park, New Delhi - 110 017, India.
Penguin Group (NZ), 67 Apollo Drive, Rosedale, North Shore 0632, New Zealand
    (a division of Pearson New Zealand Ltd).
Penguin Books (South Africa) (Pty) Ltd, 24 Sturdee Avenue, Rosebank, Johannesburg 2196, South Africa.
Penguin Books Ltd, Registered Offices: 80 Strand, London WC2R 0RL, England.

Design by Semadar Megged.   Text set in 18-point Zapf Humanist 601 BT.
The artwork is rendered in pencil and gouache on 140 lb. d'Arches rough watercolor paper.

Library of Congress Cataloging-in-Publication Data
Dunrea, Olivier.
Old Bear and his cub / Olivier Dunrea.   p. cm.   Summary: Although they love each
other, Old Bear and his Little Cub have a tug-of-war over which one knows best in a
variety of situations.   [1. Bears—Fiction. 2. Parent and child—Fiction.] I. Title.
PZ7.D922Od 2010   [E]—dc22  2008000663

ISBN 978-0-399-24507-7    10 9 8 7 6
Special Markets ISBN 978-0-399-25562-5  Not for resale

This Imagination Library edition is published by Penguin Young Readers, a division
of Penguin Random House, exclusively for Dolly Parton's Imagination Library,
a not-for-profit program designed to inspire a love of reading and learning, sponsored
in part by The Dollywood Foundation. Penguin's trade editions of this work are
available wherever books are sold.